W9-BVN-251

Oh Where, Oh Where Has My Little Dog Gone?

As told and illustrated by
Iza Trapani

REWARD
Lost dog
call 419-2597

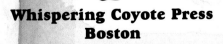

Whispering Coyote Press
Boston

Published by Whispering Coyote Press
480 Newbury Street, Suite 104, Danvers, MA 01923
Copyright © 1995 by Iza Trapani

Printed in Hong Kong by South China Printing Company (1988) Ltd.
10 9 8 7 6 5 4 3 2

Book production and design by Our House

Library of Congress Cataloging–in–Publication Data

Trapani, Iza
Oh where, oh where has my little dog gone? / written and illustrated by Iza Trapani.
p.   cm.
Summary: An expanded version of the well-known song, in which the dog runs away from
home and explores the desert, mountains, and oceans before deciding that home
is best. Includes music.
ISBN 1–879085–75–5 : $14.95
1. Children's songs—Texts. [1. Dogs—Songs and music. 2. Songs.] I. Title.
PZ8.3.T6860h 1995
782.42164—dc20   94–48811
[E]   CIP
                                                      AC

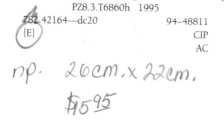

To my sister Elżbieta,
and my brother Lech, with love
      —I.T.

Oh where, oh where has my little dog gone?
Oh where, oh where can he be?
With his ears cut short and his tail cut long,
Oh where, oh where can he be?

Perhaps I shouldn't have scolded him when
He chewed a hole in my shoe.
But I had to teach my dog right from wrong.
What else was I going to do?

His feelings must have been terribly hurt.
His heart was filled with dismay.
So he packed his bowl and his favorite toy,
And then my dog ran away.

He took a bus that was headed for town.
A tourist, he thought he'd be.

But he never got past the rushing crowds,
And not one sight did he see.

"I think I'll go to the mountains," he said,
"And climb to my heart's content."
But he lost his grip on the icy slope.
Back down the mountain he went.

So next he thought he would surf in the sea.
He'd never tried it before.

But a giant wave knocked him off his feet,
And threw him back to the shore.

"I'd rather hike in the desert," he said.
"It's warm and peaceful out there."
But he tripped and fell on a rattlesnake.
It gave them both quite a scare!

"A cowboy's life is exciting," he'd heard.
"A rodeo could be fun."

But the horse he rode pitched him in the dirt.
My dog was glad to be done.

"I'm tired," he said. "I'll go sleep in a cave.
How snug and cozy I'll be."
But he didn't know that a big brown bear
Would come keep him company.

By now my doggie was hungry and weak.
The sun was setting so low.
He longed to eat and he longed to sleep,
But had no place he could go.

And then he thought of his warm, loving home,
The place he most wished to be.
With a wagging tail and a joyful heart,
He ran right back home to me.

What great adventures my little dog had,
While roaming so far away.
Though he learned a lot and is wiser now,
I think he's come home to stay!

Oh where, oh where has my lit - tle dog gone? Oh where, oh where can he be?_____ With his ears cut short and his tail cut long, Oh where, oh where can he be?_____

2. Perhaps I shouldn't have scolded him when
He chewed a hole in my shoe.
But I had to teach my dog right from wrong.
What else was I going to do?

3. His feelings must have been terribly hurt.
His heart was filled with dismay.
So he packed his bowl and his favorite toy,
And then my dog ran àway.

4. He took a bus that was headed for town.
A tourist, he thought he'd be.
But he never got past the rushing crowds,
And not one sight did he see.

5. "I think I'll go to the mountains," he said,
"And climb to my heart's content."
But he lost his grip on the icy slope.
Back down the mountain he went.

6. So next he thought he would surf in the sea.
He'd never tried it before.
But a giant wave knocked him off his feet,
And threw him back to the shore.

7. "I'd rather hike in the desert," he said.
"It's warm and peaceful out there."
But he tripped and fell on a rattlesnake.
It gave them both quite a scare!

8. "A cowboy's life is exciting," he'd heard.
"A rodeo could be fun."
But the horse he rode pitched him in the dirt.
My dog was glad to be done.

9. "I'm tired," he said. "I'll go sleep in a cave.
How snug and cozy I'll be."
But he didn't know that a big brown bear
Would come keep him company.

10. By now my doggie was hungry and weak.
The sun was setting so low.
He longed to eat and he longed to sleep,
But had no place he could go.

11. And then he thought of his warm, loving home,
The place he most wished to be.
With a wagging tail and a joyful heart,
He ran right back home to me.

12. What great adventures my little dog had,
While roaming so far away.
Though he learned a lot and is wiser now,
I think he's come home to stay!